Lila and Myla the Twins Fairies

To Greta and Emile

Special thanks to Rachel Elliot

ISBN 978-0-545-70825-8

12 11 10 9 8 7 6 5 4 3 2 1   15 16 17 18 19/0

Printed in the U.S.A.   40

First printing, January 2015

Lila and Myla the Twins Fairies

by Daisy Meadows

SCHOLASTIC INC.

The Fairyland Palace

Lila & Myla's Cottage

Tippington Town

I will not sleep nor rest my head
Till fairy hearts are filled with dread.
Soon twins around the world will find
They've left their happy days behind.

This spell makes me a work of art;
Twice as mean and twice as smart.
The king and queen will both be lost
And and will turn to frost!

**Find the hidden letters in the hearts
throughout this book. Unscramble all 7 letters
to spell a special twin word!**

Lila's Pendant

Contents

Party Pairs

"This is the one," said Rachel Walker, pointing up at a tall white town house.

A bunch of pink balloons was tied to the gate, and there was another bunch pinned to the front door. Rachel smoothed down her party dress and smiled at her best friend, Kirsty Tate. Kirsty was staying with Rachel during her school vacation.

"It was really nice of your friends to invite me to their birthday parties," said Kirsty. "I've never been to two in one day before!"

Rachel's friends Jessy and Amy were twins, and they were having two separate birthday parties—one for each of them.

"Jessy and Amy's parents are really fun," Rachel said as they walked up to the front door. "They're letting Jessy have her party this morning, and Amy have hers this afternoon. The twins like different music and decorations, and their mom and dad wanted to make sure they're both happy!"

She knocked on the door, and it opened to reveal a girl with long blonde hair and big blue eyes. She was wearing a sparkly

2

pink party dress and there was a pink
bow in her hair.

"Happy birthday, Jessy!" said Rachel.

"Thanks," said Jessy with a smile.
"This must be Kirsty. Hi!"

"Hi, and happy birthday," said Kirsty.

Jessy invited them in. There were pink balloons pinned in every corner and the guests were dancing to music. A table was piled high with presents wrapped in pink paper.

"Those are the prizes for the party games," Jessy said, seeing Rachel looking at them.

Kirsty peeked
into the
kitchen
and saw a
tray full of
pink gelatin
treats on the
dining table.

"Pink's
my favorite color,"
said Jessy. "Can you tell?"

The girls laughed and gave Jessy her
presents. Then another girl came over
and gave Rachel a hug.

"Happy birthday, Amy," said Rachel.
"Kirsty, this is Amy—Jessy's twin."

"Wow, you don't look alike!" said
Kirsty in surprise.

Amy's blonde hair was cut into a
bob, and she was wearing
cropped jeans and a
red T-shirt. She
laughed and
linked arms with
her sister.

"We're
identical twins,
but we're very
different," she
said. "Luckily,
our parents let us
be ourselves! Come on, let's start playing
some games."

The first game was musical chairs. It
was a lot of fun, but suddenly the CD
started to skip. While Jessy's dad tried to
fix it, her mom went to the prize table.

"We might as well end the game now and start on dessert," she said. "Oh, no! Where have all the prizes gone?"

The table was completely empty. Jessy's father frowned.

"Someone must have moved them," he said. "I'll go look in the kitchen."

But when he went into the kitchen, he let out a shout of surprise. Rachel and Kirsty hurried after him, followed by the rest of the party guests.

The kitchen was a terrible mess. The
bowls of beautiful pink gelatin had been
knocked upside down and trampled into
the kitchen mat. Paint and glitter from the
craft table in the corner had also been
emptied all over the floor.

While everyone was wondering
what had happened, Kirsty tugged on
Rachel's arm.

"Look over there," she whispered.

There was a large footprint in some
spilled purple glitter, and the girls
recognized it at once.

"It's a goblin footprint!" whispered
Rachel.

Jessy's dad folded his arms. He
suddenly looked very grumpy.

"If Jessy's party is going to be this
much trouble, we might have to cancel
Amy's party," he said.

"I agree," said Jessy's mom, frowning.
"Suddenly, I'm feeling very tired."

Jessy and Amy looked upset.

"Our birthday is turning into a
disaster!" cried Amy.

Seeing Double

Jessy's parents walked back into the living room and the guests followed. Rachel and Kirsty stayed back, looking puzzled.

"I've never heard Jessy's mom and dad sound so upset," Rachel said.

Just then, a green balloon floated past them toward the open back door. It bobbed out into the yard.

"That's strange," said Kirsty. "I thought that all Jessy's balloons were pink."

"They were," said Rachel. "Kirsty, do you think that there are goblins here? After all, green's their favorite color!"

Rachel and Kirsty knew all about goblins, because they were friends with the fairies. Jack Frost liked sending his goblins to cause trouble for the fairies, and Rachel and Kirsty had often helped their magical friends.

"Let's follow the balloon," said Kirsty. "If it *is* goblins, there's sure to be more trouble."

The girls ran out into the yard and spotted the balloon floating behind a wooden shed. They ran around the corner of the shed and saw a little pond.

Two garden gnomes were standing next
to it with toy fishing rods.

"Look, there's the balloon," said Rachel.
"There's
definitely
something
magical
about it."

It hovered
by the shed
wall, even
though there
was a little
breeze that
should have blown it away. As the girls
watched, it began to grow bigger and
bigger. Then . . . *POP*! The balloon
disappeared, and two tiny fairies were
fluttering toward Rachel and Kirsty!

"Hello, I'm Myla," said the fairy on the left.

"And I'm Lila," said the fairy on the right.

Rachel and Kirsty blinked, hardly able to believe their eyes. The fairies were both wearing pale orange shorts, pink jackets, and  sparkly ankle boots. They both had short black hair, but Myla had pink highlights and Lila had blue.

"We're the Twins Fairies!" they said together.

"It's wonderful to meet you both," said Kirsty.

"I'm so glad you were in the balloon," said Rachel. "We thought that the goblins might be up to something."

She described the problems they'd had at the birthday party and the goblin footprint they'd seen.

"That's why we're here," said Lila in a serious voice. "The queen sent us from Fairyland to ask for your help."

"We're always happy to help Fairyland

in any way we can," said Rachel. "What happened?"

"It's Jack Frost," said Myla, sounding gentler than her twin. "He and his goblins crept into our cottage yesterday while we were out. They stole some very precious magic objects from us."

"Without them, things are going to go terribly wrong for twins everywhere," finished Lila. "You see, we look after twins all over the human world and in Fairyland."

"Is that why things were going badly at the party?" asked Kirsty. "Presents disappeared, and the music stopped."

The twins nodded.

"It's all Jack Frost's fault," said Myla with a sigh.

"What are your magic objects?"
Rachel asked.

"First, there's the heart
pendant," said
Lila. "I have
one half, and
Myla has
the other.
My half
makes sure that
people treat twins
as individuals, and
Myla's half makes sure that
twins have fun being together."

"Jack Frost also took our Gemini ring,"
said Myla. "It ensures that twins aren't
compared with each other all the time."

"Will you help us find our magic
objects?" asked Lila.

Of course," said Kirsty at once. "But
ow are we—"

She broke off when she heard a
strange, high-pitched giggle coming from
the pond.

"Look!" cried Rachel, pointing to where
they had seen the garden gnomes fishing.
"One of the gnomes has disappeared!"

"No, he hasn't . . ." said Lila.

She swooped down
to some tall grass
next to the
pond and
pushed it
aside. A
goblin was
crouching
down
behind it.

"That wasn't a gnome at all," Kirsty exclaimed. "It was a goblin in disguise!"

The goblin leaped over the tall grass and raced away from them.

"Follow that goblin!" cried Lila.

Rachel and Kirsty looked at each other in surprise. They'd never seen a goblin run so fast!

Tricked!

The girls raced after the goblin, who darted into the garden shed and slammed the door shut. Rachel pushed on the door, but it wouldn't open.

"I think he's leaning against the door," she said.

"We need to ask him what he knows about our magic objects," said Myla.

"If we all push together, we might be stronger than him," said Kirsty. "Let's try."

Rachel and Kirsty pushed on the shed door with all their strength. Myla and Lila pushed, too, fluttering as hard as they could against the top of the door.

They heard a squawk from inside, then the door gave way and they all tumbled inside.

"There he is!" cried Lila.

The goblin was trying to hide under an old umbrella.

"We can see you," said Kirsty. "Please come out of there—we just want to ask you some questions."

The goblin threw the umbrella to one side and sat down on an upturned flowerpot. He folded his arms and looked very grumpy.

"I'm not talking to humans or fairies," he said. "You're all the same. Tricky!"

"We just want to know why Jack Frost took Lila and Myla's magic objects," she said.

"And where he's hidden them," added Kirsty hopefully.

"I'm not going to tell you," said the goblin.

He stuck out his tongue and stood up.

"Let me leave," he said. "I want to go and eat more of those gelatin treats."

"There are no treats left," said Rachel. "Besides, we're not moving until you answer our questions."

The goblin sat down again and stroked his chin thoughtfully.

"Let me think . . ." he muttered.

The girls waited. Myla and Lila fluttered above them, staring hopefully at the goblin. He opened his mouth, but then closed it again. Then they all heard the town clock chime. The goblin put his head to one side as if he was counting. The clock chimed twelve times, and then the goblin giggled.

"Twelve o'clock," he said, rubbing his hands together with glee. "My job is done."

"What do you mean?" Lila demanded.

"Jack Frost has had enough of you fairies interfering with his plans," said the goblin. "I just had to make sure that you didn't take the humans to Fairyland until after twelve o'clock. That way, Jack Frost knew you would be too late to stop him!"

Lila and Myla groaned, but Kirsty had an idea.

"You were very smart to trick us like that," she said to the goblin. "You had us completely fooled."

"I'm the best actor of all the goblins in the Ice Castle," boasted the goblin.

"I bet Jack Frost told you all about his plans," Kirsty went on. "I'm sure he shared them with a smart goblin like you."

"Oh, yes, I know everything," said the goblin with a smug smile.

"Go ahead and tell us," said Kirsty. "After all, it doesn't matter now. You kept us here past twelve o'clock."

"That's true," said the goblin cheerfully. "From now on, it's going to be *twice* as hard for you to get the better of Jack Frost!"

"What do you mean?" asked Myla.

"He stole the magic objects so that he could make his *own* twin," said the goblin, looking up at the fairies with a smirk. "Two Jack Frosts will be able to take over Fairyland forever!"

Myla gasped, and Lila let out a shocked cry.

"Can he do that?" asked Rachel.

"Our magic objects are very powerful," said Myla. "If he combines his magic with ours, he can use it to make a copy of himself."

"*Two* Jack Frosts?" said Kirsty. "One is bad enough—how will we be able to stop two?"

"Let's go to the Ice Castle," said Lila, raising her wand. "Maybe Jack Frost won't know how to use our magic. If we're lucky, we might still be in time to stop him!"

Twice the Ice

Lila and Myla put their wands together, and a double jet of pink fairy dust spiraled out. The glittering swirl wound around Rachel and Kirsty, lifting them into the air and shrinking them until they were fairy-size. They felt glimmering wings grow on their backs, and then they were fluttering together up near the roof of the shed.

"It's pointless," called the goblin, gazing up at them. "You can't stop him now."

"We'll see about that!" said Lila.

The fairies tapped their wands together twice, and Rachel and Kirsty were surrounded by a starburst of fairy dust. When the sparkles cleared, they were fluttering above the Ice Castle. Snow blanketed the ground, but for once the sun was shining, and the girls were very warm.

"I can see Jack Frost!" said Kirsty immediately. "Look, he's in the main courtyard with all the goblins."

"Let's hide in one of the turrets and watch," said Rachel.

The girls had both been to the Ice Castle before, so they led Myla and Lila to a turret from where they could see the courtyard.

Jack Frost was standing in the middle of a group of goblins.

"I can only see one Jack Frost," Myla whispered. "Maybe his spell didn't work."

He was strutting up and down in front of something that was tall and thin, and covered in a red cloth.

"You are very lucky goblins," Jack Frost declared. "You are about to witness my greatest triumph!"

"Get your wand ready," Lila whispered to her twin. "When he casts his spell, we have to try to block it. If we work together, we should be strong enough to stop him."

But instead of raising his wand, he raised his hand and pulled off the red cover. Standing on a round platform was an exact copy of Jack Frost. The spell had already been done!

"My name is Jimmy Thaw," announced the twin. "I have come to rule over you, side by side with my brother, Jack!"

The fairies gasped, and several of the goblins squawked and screeched. One

of them fainted, and several others
scrambled to hide. Jack Frost cackled
with pleasure.

"Behold the power of my magic!"
he said as Jimmy Thaw waved to the
crowd of goblins and grinned at him.
"I should thank those who have helped
me—I couldn't have done it without
Lila and Myla!"

"How could he say that?" cried Myla, her eyes filling with tears. "We didn't help him!"

Lila put her arms around her twin and gave her a warm hug.

"We're going to stop him and get our magic objects back," she said. "We have Rachel and Kirsty to help us, so try not to worry."

Rachel and Kirsty exchanged nervous smiles. They hoped that they could live up to Lila's belief in them!

Just then, Jack Frost jabbed his finger at a nearby goblin, who was staring at the new twin with his mouth hanging open.

"What are you waiting for?" Jack Frost bellowed. "Go and hide that fairy trinket *now*!"

The goblin squealed in alarm and sprinted out of the castle.

"Look, he's got something in his hand!" said Rachel.

"It must be one of our magic objects," Myla exclaimed, brushing her tears away. "Come on, let's follow him!"

Magical Mimics

Led by Myla, the fairies zoomed out
of the turret and followed the goblin
as he ran away from the castle. They
flew higher up and saw him racing
toward the forest.

"We'll have to fly lower or else we'll
lose him among the trees," called Kirsty.

In single file, the fairies swooped down
and followed the goblin into the forest.

The sun had been making the snow-covered branches sparkle, but now that they were inside the forest, everything was dark and cold.

"I can hear the goblin up ahead," whispered Rachel. "Listen!"

There was a loud crashing and crunching up ahead, as if the goblin was stumbling through thick bushes and losing his way. They flew as fast as they could, weaving through spiky branches, trying to keep up with him. Suddenly, the crashing noises stopped.

"Oh, no. I hope we haven't lost him," said Myla.

"No, don't worry," said Lila, who was in the lead. "He stopped to catch his breath."

There was a little clearing up ahead, and the goblin sat on a boulder, huffing and puffing. The girls could see a delicate chain dangling from his hand and something  dark pink clutched in his fist.

"That's my half of the pendant!" Lila exclaimed. "Myla has the pale pink half, and mine is dark pink."

"How can we get it back?" asked Myla, worried.

"Jack Frost's spell gave me an idea," said Rachel. "Maybe if we all look like exact copies of the goblin, we can confuse him into giving us back the pendant."

Myla and Lila looked at each other and nodded.

"We think that's a fantastic idea," said Myla.

Rachel and Kirsty couldn't help but laugh at their reaction.

"Can you read each other's minds?" asked Kirsty.

"No," said Lila with a grin. "But we are so close that often we just know what the other is thinking!"

Myla and Lila linked their little fingers

and raised their wands at exactly the same time. Then they chanted the spell together:

*"To stop Jack Frost
from causing trouble,
make each of us
the goblin's double!"*

A rush of icy wind ruffled the girls' hair and made them shiver. Then their ears became pointy, their noses began to grow, and their skin turned a pale shade of green. Within a few seconds, they all looked exactly the same as the goblin in the clearing.

"Let me go first," said Rachel. "I'm going to annoy him by copying everything he does."

She crept closer to the goblin and waited until he was looking down. Then she moved right in front of him. The goblin stood up and then jumped. Rachel jumped, too.

"That's funny," he said to himself. "I don't remember seeing a mirror here before."

He moved his arms, and Rachel copied everything he did. Then Kirsty ran into the clearing and started to do a wild dance.

"Another mirror." The goblin gasped. "But this one's making me look silly! Stop it! I would never dance like that!"

Lila did a somersault into the clearing and then jumped up and made the craziest face she could manage.

"EEK!" squealed the goblin. "I don't do somersaults, and I don't look like that! I'm tall, green, and handsome! Take these mirrors away! I don't like them!"

He started to back away, but he bumped into Myla.

"BOO!" she said when he turned around in surprise.

"Help!" squealed the goblin, waving his hands in the air.

All four copies started waving their hands in the air, too, and shouting "Help! Help!" just like him. Finally, the goblin flung the pendant down on the ground and kicked it away from him.

"I've had enough of this terrible twin magic!" he howled. "I'm leaving!"

With a final squeal of alarm, he ran
back into the forest. Lila and Myla
swished their wands and turned them
all back into fairies. Then Lila fluttered
down, picked up her half of the pendant,
and fastened it around her neck.

"Hooray!" cheered Myla, hugging her
twin. "Now Jack Frost can't make any
more copies of himself."

Rachel and Kirsty clapped, and then they all held hands and danced into the air, twirling around in a glimmering fairy circle. It was lots of fun, but when they floated to the ground again, Lila looked serious.

"It's wonderful that we got my pendant back, but we still need Myla's half and the Gemini ring to be able to help twins again," she said.

"Then we have to keep looking," said Rachel in a determined voice. "Don't worry, Myla. We'll find your pendant and stop Jack Frost's plans. I know we will!"

Myla's Pendant

Contents

An Icy Classroom

Myla looked hopefully at Rachel and Kirsty. "Thanks for your help, girls. I really need my pendant back!"

"We have to stop Jack Frost from causing any more problems," said Kirsty.

"He'll be planning all kinds of trouble now that he has his own twin," Rachel added solemnly.

With a determined nod, Lila zoomed up through the dense trees.

"Come on!" she called over her shoulder. "If we go back to the Ice Castle, we might find a clue to where he's hidden our other magic objects!"

The castle turrets were topped with snow, and gray clouds hovered overhead. But when the friends reached the courtyard, the huge crowd of goblins had disappeared. There were just a few goblin guards leaning against the courtyard wall, arguing. The fairies

fluttered together and Rachel pointed to
an opening on one side of the courtyard.
A guard was standing next to it,
yawning.

"That's the way to the throne room,"
Rachel whispered. "I remember from
when we were here before."

"But how are we going to get past the
guard?" asked Kirsty.

"I have an idea," said Lila with a twinkle in her eyes. "He looks a little sleepy, don't you think?"

Myla giggled and raised her wand.

"Sometimes it really does seem like Lila and I can read each other's minds," she told the girls.

She waved her wand and cast a silent spell. A little stream of shimmering fairy dust coiled out of her wand and wound around the goblin guard's head. He yawned and then slid down the wall, fast asleep. Rachel and Kirsty had to

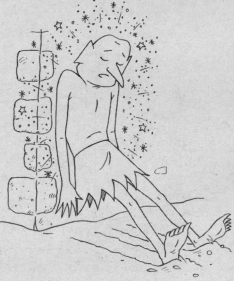

put their hands over their mouths to stifle their giggles!

"Lead the way to the throne room," Lila whispered to them. "We have to find Jack Frost."

Rachel and Kirsty zoomed into the dark entrance, followed by Lila and Myla. They fluttered through a maze of damp, smelly corridors, hearing only the steady drip of water.

At last they reached the door of the throne room. It was slightly ajar, and someone inside was shouting loudly.

"That's Jack Frost," Kirsty whispered.

"That's all wrong!" he bellowed. "You'll be in detention for a month if you don't get this right! Now, you have one more chance. What do you do when you see a fairy?"

"Ask them if they'd like a cup of tea?" suggested a friendly voice.

"If you see a fairy, you steal her magic

objects!" Jack Frost roared. "Repeat after me:

When you and I rule Fairyland,
all pesky fairies will be banned!"

Myla beckoned to the others and slipped through the opening into the throne room. Lila was close behind her, followed by Rachel and Kirsty. A wooden chair stood next to the door, and each of them hid behind one of its legs. Then they gazed around in amazement.

61

The throne room had been decorated to look like a classroom. There was a large desk in front of the throne, and Jack Frost was wearing a cap and gown. Jimmy Thaw sat at a small desk facing the throne. The goblins sat in neat rows on the floor behind him.

"What's so bad about fairies?" asked Jimmy Thaw.

Jack Frost thumped the desk in front of him, and his cap slipped to one side.

"We're not leaving this room until you agree to help me take over Fairyland!" he shouted.

Fairies in Hiding

The goblins started to complain.

"I'm hungry!" squawked one.

"The floor's too hard!" cried another.

Jimmy Thaw turned to look at them. "Poor things," he said. "Let's stop for a snack and find some cushions for them to sit on."

The goblins gazed at him with adoring eyes, but Jack Frost turned purple with fury.

"No snacks!" he shouted. "No cushions!"

Lila turned to the others, her eyes sparkling with fun.

"It looks like Jack Frost isn't enjoying having a twin as much as he expected!" she whispered.

Jack Frost took a deep breath.

"Listen," he said, "You're not here to talk about cushions."

"Of course not," said Jimmy Thaw in a polite voice. "I'm glad to hear you say that, because there are a few other things I'd like to talk about."

"Yes," said Jack Frost, rubbing his hands together and snickering. "There's lots of plotting and planning to be done."

"I'm good at planning," said Jimmy
Thaw. "First, I think the whole castle
needs a coat of paint. We should turn on
the heat, too—it's a little chilly."

Jack Frost's mouth dropped open, but
his twin didn't seem to notice.

"I'd also like to talk about raises for
the goblins," Jimmy Frost
continued.

The goblins
shuffled closer
and closer to
Jimmy Thaw.
One very small
goblin sat on
his foot.

"I love you,"
whispered the little
goblin.

Jimmy Thaw patted him on the head and Jack Frost scowled, pulling at something around his neck.

"*I'm* his twin," the fairies heard Jack Frost mutter. "He should like *me* the best."

"I think he's jealous," said Rachel.

"Look!" whispered Kirsty. "He's taking off something from his neck."

Myla gasped in excitement.

"It's my half of the pendant!" she said.

Jack Frost held up the pendant and then put it around Jimmy Thaw's neck.

"This is a present for you," he said. "But you can never take it off, and must always keep it safe from the fairies."

"Thank you very much!" said Jimmy Thaw.

Kirsty turned to the others.

"This is our chance," she whispered. "Jimmy Thaw seems really nice. If we explain to him that  the pendant is stolen, maybe he will return it."

Rachel, Lila, and Myla nodded, but then Jack Frost spoke again.

"We'll continue your meanness lessons later," he said with a scowl. "Goblins, look after my twin and give him whatever he wants, OR ELSE!"

"He's coming this way!" Myla squeaked excitedly.

As Jack Frost strode past the fairies' hiding place, his flowing cloak caught Rachel's wings and knocked her down. She tumbled out from under the chair— right into the middle of the room!

Luckily, no one seemed to see her. The goblins were all gazing at Jimmy Thaw, and he was looking at the pendant around his neck. Rachel was safe. She zoomed into the air, and the others flew up to join her.

"How are we going to talk to Jimmy Thaw in private?" asked Myla. "Those goblins don't want to leave his side!"

They all peered down at the group below them. They had to come up with a plan—fast!

Distracted Goblins

Just then, Jimmy Thaw stood up and yawned.

"I'm tired," he said. "I think I'll go to my room for a little snooze."

The fairies looked around at one another hopefully.

"Maybe this could be our chance," Lila whispered.

But the goblins stood up, too.

"We'll come with you," said the smallest goblin.

The procession set off though the castle. There were two goblins walking ahead of Jimmy Thaw, two next to him, and two behind him. The fairies fluttered along above their heads, trying to think of a way to speak to Jimmy Thaw alone.

After they followed the procession along three corridors and up two flights of stairs, Lila groaned.

"This is impossible!" she said. "The goblins are never going to leave him alone."

"Maybe we can *tempt* them away from him somehow," said Rachel.

"Good thinking, Rachel," said Myla. "I've got an idea!"

She waved her wand, and two green yo-yos rolled out of the shadows toward the last goblins in the procession.

They stopped and picked them up.

"I'm fantastic at yo-yoing," said one.

"Not as good as me!" said the other.

Glaring at each other, the goblins started a yo-yo competition. They forgot all about following the others.

"That was great, Myla," said Kirsty with a giggle.

"Watch this!" said Lila.

She waved her wand, and two delicious-smelling pastries appeared on a plate at the edge of the corridor. Lila sent the smell drifting toward the two goblins next to Jimmy Thaw in the procession. They stopped and sniffed the air.

"What's that?" whispered one.

"Look!" said the other, pointing at the pastries. "Yummy!"

They scurried over to the pastries and started to gobble them up.

"Four down, two to go," said Rachel. "What should we try next?"

"Lila, could you make me sound like Jack Frost?" Kirsty suggested. "I have an idea."

Lila winked and waved her wand. "Did it work?" she asked.

"How do I sound?" whispered Kirsty.

The others giggled.

"You sound exactly like Jack Frost!" said Lila.

"Except we're not used to hearing Jack Frost whisper," Rachel added.

Kirsty grinned and fluttered down until she was flying along next to the ear of one of the goblins. It was so dark in the corridor that he didn't see her.

"You, goblin!" she said in Jack Frost's voice. "Get back to the throne room and polish my desk!"

The goblin jumped and scurried back toward the throne room. Kirsty flew back to join the others, smiling, and Lila returned her voice to normal. Jimmy

Thaw and his goblin companion
walked straight ahead to the door of
a turret bedroom.

"This is my room," said Jimmy Thaw.
"Time for a little nap."

The fairies followed Jimmy Thaw
and the goblin into the bedroom. Jimmy
Thaw sat on the end of the bed, and
Myla groaned. The goblin wasn't going
to leave him alone!

A Sleepy Song

"Can you girls try to distract the goblin so we can talk to Jimmy Thaw?" asked Lila.

"We'll do our best!" whispered Rachel.

While Jimmy Thaw stretched and plumped up his pillows, the goblin yawned and sank into an uncomfortable-looking chair next to the window. Rachel and Kirsty hid in a fold of the curtain behind him.

"He's not taking his eyes off Jimmy Thaw," said Rachel.

"Do you remember the sleeping spell that Myla cast earlier?" Kirsty whispered. "Maybe we could try that."

"But we can't do magic," said Rachel.

"No," agreed Kirsty, "but maybe he'll drop off to sleep if we sing him a lullaby!"

From behind the curtain, the girls began to sing in soft voices. The goblin's eyelids drooped, flickered, and drooped again. Rachel and Kirsty kept singing, and at last the goblin's eyes closed.

"He's asleep!" said Rachel.

Together with Lila and Myla, they fluttered out in front of Jimmy Thaw, who was just settling back onto his pillows.

"Why, hello!" he exclaimed. "Are you fairies?"

"Yes," said Lila. "We're the Twins Fairies, and these are our friends Rachel and Kirsty. We've come to ask you to return something that belongs to us."

Quickly, the fairies told Jimmy Thaw
how Jack Frost had stolen their magic
objects. Jimmy Thaw's eyes opened
very wide and he touched the pendant
around his neck.

"You're saying that this necklace is
stolen?" he asked.

"Yes," said Rachel. "It belongs to
Myla. Lila has the other half—look."

Lila showed him her half of the
pendant.

"Well, if this belongs to you, then of course you can have it back," he said at once. "But I think there must be some sort of misunderstanding. I can't believe my twin would take something that didn't belong to him."

"He's done it before, and so have his goblins," said Kirsty.

"There's only one thing we can do," said Jimmy Thaw, standing up. "We're going to find Jack and ask him for an explanation!"

"Please don't go to Jack Frost!" cried Rachel. "He can't know we're here!"

"He'll try to capture us!" said Myla.

"No, no," said Jimmy Thaw, waving
his hand. "He's just joking when he says
things like that. Don't worry, we'll soon
get this cleared up and then we'll all
have a nice cup of hot cocoa."

He marched out of the room, and the
fairies darted after him.
They sped through
the corridors and
down the stairs,
pleading with
him to stop.
But when he
reached the
throne room
door, he pushed
it open and strode
inside.

Jack Frost was sitting on his throne, but he jumped to his feet when he saw his twin and the fairies.

"What's going on?" he bellowed.

"There seems to have been a little mix-up," said Jimmy Thaw. "These fairies say that the pendant you gave me belongs to them. I'm sure you can explain everything."

Jack Frost clenched his fists. "Of course I can explain!" he yelled. "I took it, so it's MINE!"

Jimmy Thaw stared at him in shock. "But stealing is wrong," he said.

He took the pendant from around his neck and held it out to Myla. Jack Frost let out a howl of anger as Myla took it and placed it around her neck.

"You might have it now, but you won't keep it!" said Jack Frost, glaring at the fairies. "Goblins, don't let any of them out of this room!"

Myla looked over at her twin in alarm. How were they going to get home?

Jimmy Thaw Takes a Side

Some of the goblins raced across the room to block the doorway, while others leaped into the air to try to catch the fairies. Rachel, Kirsty, Lila, and Myla fluttered out of their reach.

"Try the windows!" called Lila.

They zoomed around the room, but all the windows were closed. Fluttering above the goblins' grasping hands, they looked at each other, worried.

"We can't get out," said Rachel. "What are we going to do?"

Jack Frost looked up at them, and a mean smile spread across his face.

"I'll make you a deal," he said. "I'll let you go if you give me the pendant."

"Never!" squeaked Myla.

"No way!" added her twin, folding her arms across her chest.

"Then you'll never leave my throne room!" Jack Frost yelled. "Goblins, get that pendant!"

The goblins climbed on each other's shoulders, creating living ladders that swayed across the room. The fairies were forced to press themselves against the ceiling, but the goblins just kept climbing and making

more ladders. The room was filling up with them.

"There's no escape!" cried Kirsty.

"Goblins," said a gentle voice. "Dear goblins, please listen to me."

It was Jimmy Thaw. The goblins turned to look at him. Two of them lost their balance, and they all fell over.

"You are all tired and hungry," he said. "Why waste your energy trying to catch these poor little fairies? Let's all go to the kitchen and have a feast!"

The goblins cheered, but Jack Frost stamped his foot.

"If you let those fairies go, I'll punish you all for a YEAR!" he shouted.

"Forget about the fairies, and ignore my grumpy twin," Jimmy Thaw told the goblins. "This is my home, too, and I say it's feast time. Come on, goblins— let the fairies go!"

With whoops and cheers, the goblins darted around the room, flinging open the windows.

"Go!" cried Jimmy Thaw to the fairies. "Good luck!"

"Thank you!" called the fairies.

One by one, they swooped out through a window. In a few seconds, Rachel, Kirsty, Lila, and Myla were hovering high above the Ice Castle.  The angry yells of Jack Frost and the excited squeals of the goblins were ringing in their ears.

"We did it!" cheered Lila, spinning around in delight. "Now we have both halves of the pendant. Hooray!"

"That means everything should be back to normal at your friend's party," said Myla to the girls. "We'll send you back so that you can enjoy the fun."

"But what about the Gemini ring?" asked Rachel. "Jack Frost still has that."

"We'll come and find you soon to help us look for it," Lila promised. "But now it's party time for you!"

She waved her wand, and there was a dazzling flash of sparkling light. When the sparkles cleared, Rachel and Kirsty were back in Jessy and Amy's yard. They could hear happy shouts and laughter coming from the house.

"Of course, no time has passed since we left," said Kirsty. "That's one of the best things about visiting Fairyland!"

"Come on," said Rachel. "Let's go and see if finding the pendants has made a difference."

They ran up to the house and hurried
back through the kitchen into the living
room. Everyone was getting ready to play
Pass the Present, and Jessy smiled at them.

"Come and join the game," she said.
"Mom and Dad found the missing
prizes—someone had moved them by
mistake."

"And there are still going to be two parties," added her mom with a smile. "I don't know what made us even think about canceling one!"

Rachel and Kirsty shared a secret glance as they sat down. They knew exactly what had gone wrong!

"I hope we can find the Gemini ring soon," Kirsty whispered. "Without it, there could still be trouble at Amy's party."

The music began and the present started to make its way around the circle. Rachel squeezed Kirsty's hand.

"I'm sure we'll be able to help," she said. "But right now we've got a party game to play!"

The Gemini Ring

Contents

Brand-new Twins

"Higher!" shouted Kirsty, in between giggles.

Rachel pushed her tree swing again and Kirsty flew into the air.

"Your feet touched the branches!" said Rachel, laughing.

"Higher!" Kirsty urged.

Rachel pushed as hard as she could, and Kirsty flew into the air again. This time, she seemed to stay up for a long time. When she came down, there was a flurry of golden sparkles, and Myla and Lila were hovering above her!

"We've got some news!" said Myla in an excited voice.

She flew away from Kirsty and perched on Rachel's shoulder.

"There's a big twins research conference starting today," said Lila.

110

"They're holding a garden party, and there will be lots of twins there."

"Oh, dear," said Kirsty. "Without the Gemini ring, that could be a disaster."

"Exactly," said Myla. "But this afternoon, Jimmy Thaw came to the Fairyland Palace."

"What did he want?" asked Rachel.

"He came to tell us that Jack Frost is

going to the conference to try to find out how to make the two of them more alike," said Lila. "But Jimmy Thaw doesn't want to be like him, so he has promised to meet us there and help us get the ring back!"

"That's wonderful!" Kirsty exclaimed, jumping down from the swing. "Let's go!"

"We hoped you'd say that," said Myla, fluttering into the air. "Ready, Lila?"

In perfect unison, the Twins Fairies raised their wands and waved them in figure eights.

There was a burst of glimmering
fairy dust, and then
Rachel and
Kirsty heard
a whooshing
sound. They
blinked,
and found
themselves
standing at
the entrance gate
of a large garden,
next to a big sign.

TWINS CONFERENCE GARDEN PARTY
Research scientists and twins only!

"Oh, no," said Myla. "How can Kirsty
and Rachel get inside?"

"You could turn us into fairies," Kirsty
suggested.

"I've got a better idea," said
Lila. "How about you
and Rachel
become twins?"

Rachel and
Kirsty exchanged
a thrilled glance.

"Yes, please!"
they said
together.

Lila laughed.

"You're already
starting to sound like twins!"
she said, raising her wand. "Come
on, Myla."

Together, the fairies spoke the words of
a very special spell:

Peas in pods and mirrors bright,
match these girls in looks and height.
Copy every lock of hair,
and make them seem a perfect pair.

The girls were transformed in the twinkling of an eye. They stared at each other in amazement.

"We've both got your ponytail," said Kirsty with a giggle.

"But our hair is dark like yours," said
Rachel, smiling.

Rachel was wearing a striped top and
Kirsty had a matching striped skirt.
Their shoes were exactly the same, and
over their shoulders hung matching bags.

They squeezed each other's hands and shared a smile. Just then, one of the conference organizers hurried past them.

"Come with me, twins!" he said. "You'll be late for the party!"

Twin Tempers

Lila hid inside Rachel's bag and Myla slipped into Kirsty's. Then the girls hurried into the private garden. There were rows of neatly clipped hedges and several beautifully arranged flower beds.

"I hear voices," said Kirsty.

There was a loud buzz of chatter coming from the center of the garden. Rachel and Kirsty hurried toward the sound. In the middle of the garden was a pretty little square surrounded by trees. A small crowd of people chatted and

sipped drinks. Waiters and waitresses walked around with trays of snacks.

"Look at all the twins!" said Rachel with a gasp.

Each pair of twins was dressed in the same clothes. It was amazing to see a double of everyone!

"Those must be the scientists," said Kirsty, looking at a few people dressed in suits. "None of them seems to have a twin."

"Let's join the party," said Rachel.

They walked up to a group of twins who were chatting with a scientist.

"So, you don't like being twins?" said the scientist, looking surprised.

"Everyone compares us to each other," moaned one boy.

"People don't treat us as individuals," complained a girl.

"We always have to share everything," grumbled her twin. "It's really annoying."

Lila popped her head out of Rachel's

 shoulder bag. "These twins should be excited to take part in the conference," she whispered. "They are feeling unhappy because our Gemini ring is still missing. We have to find it or the conference will be ruined!"

The girls walked on and heard a
different scientist talking to a couple of
adult twins.

"The truth is that you are smarter than
your twin," he said to one of them.

Myla peeked out of Kirsty's bag and
gasped in shock.

"No one should ever say that to

twins!" she exclaimed. "A scientist should know better. It must be because of the missing ring. Oh, dear. What are we going to do?"

"Without the ring, twins will be compared with each other all the time," said Lila. "That will make them miserable."

Rachel and Kirsty could tell how anxious Lila and Myla were feeling.

"Please don't worry," said Kirsty. "Remember, Jimmy Thaw promised to help us. We will get the ring back and stop Jack Frost's scheme."

Just then,
Rachel let out
a squeak of
excitement.
"I can see
Jack Frost!"
she said.
"He's over
there by the
statue, talking to
one of the scientists."

Next to a marble statue of a
dolphin, Jack Frost stood very close to
a scientist. She had her back against a
hedge, but she couldn't get any farther
away from him. It was obvious that
she wanted to escape. Jimmy Thaw
waited a few steps away, looking very
embarrassed.

"Let's get closer," said Kirsty. "We might be able to hear what he's saying."

They edged closer, trying to stay out of Jack Frost's view. But he only had eyes for the scientist.

"Listen to me," he was saying in a loud voice, "I'm sick of my twin being different from me. I want us to be exactly the same, and you are going to tell me how."

"But—but—but . . ." the scientist stammered.

Kirsty caught Jimmy Thaw's eye and he gave her a small smile. Then he pointed to his little finger and to Jack Frost.

"What does he mean?" Rachel whispered to Lila.

"I know!" said the fairy in an excited voice. "He means that Jack Frost has the Gemini ring on his little finger. It's here!"

Lila looked thrilled, but Myla still seemed worried. Now that they knew where the ring was, they needed to figure out how to get it back!

An Icy Prison

"I really have to go and speak to someone about . . . um . . . something . . ." said the scientist.

She ducked under Jack Frost's arm and hurried off into the crowd. Jack Frost turned, and the girls darted behind a hedge. They saw him turn on Jimmy Thaw and poke him in the chest with one long finger.

"I'm going to find a scientist who can turn you into me, even if it takes all day!" he shouted. "There's something wrong with you and the way you keep talking about being nice to fairies!"

Jimmy Thaw hung his head and looked miserable.

"Why does Jack Frost have to be so mean?" asked Myla.

Her eyes brimmed with tears of pity for Jimmy Thaw, and Lila suddenly shot up into the air.

"I won't let him upset anyone anymore,"

she said in a fierce voice. "Wait here—
I'm going to get our ring back!"

Before anyone could stop her, Lila was
zooming toward Jack Frost. She hovered
behind the statue so that no one else at
the party could see her. Then she folded
her arms and
glared at him.

"Give
back our
ring," she
demanded.
"It doesn't
belong
to you."

Jack Frost
narrowed
his eyes
into slits.

"I don't take orders from fairies!" he
snarled. He raised his wand and hurled
an ice bolt at Lila. She dodged it, but he
blasted another one and it hit her with a
blue flash. Her wand flew into the air
and Jack Frost caught it.

"No!" cried Myla.

Lila was trapped inside a tiny cage
of ice, no bigger than an egg. She shook

the freezing
bars, but
they were
too strong
for her little
hands.

"Let me
go!" she
exclaimed.
The ice
cage dropped
into Jack Frost's
hand, and he slipped it and Lila's wand
into his pocket.

"That'll teach those pesky fairies a
lesson!" he told Jimmy Thaw.

Rachel and Kirsty could hardly believe
what they had just seen. Myla was very
upset. She started to shiver.

135

"We have to rescue Lila," she cried. "She's cold in that ice cage—I can feel it, too."

"How can we get her back without Jack Frost seeing us?" asked Rachel.

"We can't," said Kirsty. "We have to be smart about it. I have an idea. Myla, can you make me look like one of the scientists?"

Myla seemed surprised, but she nodded and waved her wand. Kirsty's striped outfit was replaced by a dark blue suit, and her hair was pulled back into a bun. Thick-framed glasses disguised her face.

"What's your plan?" asked Rachel.

"No time to explain," said Kirsty. "I have to try to set Lila free."

She hurried over to Jack Frost and tapped him on the shoulder. He turned and scowled at her.

"I couldn't help overhearing you earlier," she said, trying not to sound too nervous. "I think I can help."

Jack Frost grabbed her shoulder in a tight grip.

"You can make my twin exactly the same as me?"

"I can make everything as it should be," said Kirsty. "I just need to use my special scanner."

She put her hand into her pocket and glanced over to Myla's hiding place.

Kirsty needed something that looked like a scanner—quickly! She hoped Myla would understand what she needed. Jack Frost was starting to look suspicious.

Two of a Kind

Fortunately, Myla understood. She waved her wand, and a small, square piece of metal appeared in Kirsty's hand. It bleeped and flashed with green lights. It looked very important. Kirsty held it out in front of her and ran it up and down Jack Frost's body. Then she did the same to Jimmy Thaw.

"Aha! I see," she said.

"What is it?" demanded Jack Frost. "Tell me!"

"My scanner tells me that something is stopping you from connecting as twins should," she said. "There is something very powerful about the ring you are wearing on your finger."

Jack Frost narrowed his eyes and put his hand behind his back to hide the magic Gemini ring.

"You can't have it," he snapped.

"Goodness, of course not!" said Kirsty, sounding as shocked as she could. "It doesn't belong to me, so that would be stealing. No, all you need to do is put the ring on your twin's finger. Then he will share its power."

Jack Frost's eyes lit up with excitement, and he started to tug at the ring.

"There's just one other thing," said Kirsty in a casual voice. "When you hand over the ring, make sure that you are not carrying anything very cold, like an ice cube. That could stop the ring from working the right way."

Jack Frost thrust his hand into his pocket, pulled out the ice cage, and shoved it into Kirsty's hand, along with the tiny wand.

"Hold that," he said.

Kirsty held it, not daring to release Lila until the ring was safe. Jack Frost pulled the ring off his finger and gave it to Jimmy Thaw.

"Put it on!" he ordered.

Jimmy Thaw looked around and Kirsty drew in her breath. Of course, he didn't recognize her! The last time he saw her she had been a fairy, and now she was

in disguise. Jimmy Thaw started to put
the ring on his finger and Kirsty bit her
lip. As soon as Jack Frost realized that it
wasn't working, he would want the ring
back. Her plan was going to fail!

"Wait!" cried a tiny voice.

Myla darted out of
her hiding place
and zoomed
above Jimmy
Thaw's head.
He looked up
with a smile,
and Jack Frost
flapped his hands
at her.

"Shoo, fairy pest!"
he said. "You're too late!"

"Oh, no she isn't," said his twin.

He held the ring
high above his
head, and Myla
swooped down
and took it.
Immediately, it
shrank to fairy size,
and Myla slipped it
onto her finger.

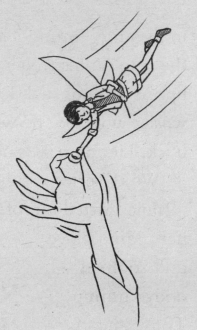

"NO!" shrieked
Jack Frost.

Just then, Lila fluttered into the air,
taking out her wand and shaking drops
of water from her wings. The warmth of
Kirsty's hand had melted her prison. Jack
Frost's eyes looked as if they might pop
out of his head. He jumped up and down
on the spot, his fists clenched. Rachel

came out of her hiding place, and Jack
Frost's eyes widened.

"What's going on?" he asked in a
choked voice.

With a wave of Myla's wand, Kirsty
and Rachel were transformed back into
their normal selves.

"YOU!" sputtered Jack Frost.

"Yes, it's us," said Rachel. "You should know by now that whenever you cause trouble for the fairies, we won't be far away."

"You told me that my twin would share the ring's power if I gave it to him," Jack Frost said to Kirsty angrily. "You lied!"

"No, I told the truth," said Kirsty in a firm voice. "Jimmy Thaw *did* share the ring's power—with its rightful owners!"

Jack Frost frowned. "It's not fair!" he cried, stomping his foot. He turned away from the girls and folded his arms.

Good-byes

Myla and Lila hugged each other, and Rachel and Kirsty jumped up and down in celebration. Now that the fairies had their magic objects back, everything would go back to normal for twins around the world.

"There's just one thing left to do," said Lila, looking sadly at Jimmy Thaw. "We have to send you back to where you came from."

"What does that mean?" asked Rachel. "Where do you come from?"

"Why," said Jimmy Thaw, "I come from Jack Frost."

"But that means you won't exist anymore," said Kirsty. "Can't you stay?"

Jimmy Thaw shook his head kindly.

"I don't belong here," he said. "But it's all right. I am a part of Jack Frost— do you understand what that means?"

The girls shook their heads.

"It means that Jack Frost isn't all bad," said Myla with a smile. "Jimmy Thaw is always somewhere inside his heart!"

Together, Myla and Lila waved their wands. Jimmy Thaw became a turquoise, twinkling blur of light, which coiled through the air and disappeared into Jack Frost's chest.

"I liked having a twin!" wailed Jack Frost.

There was a bright flash of lightning and Jack Frost disappeared, still scowling.

The girls hugged each other and smiled at the fairies, who fluttered to their shoulders.

"Listen," said Myla in a low voice.

The chatter from the conference guests suddenly sounded brighter. The twins were smiling and laughing, and Rachel and Kirsty could hear odd pieces of conversation.

"Being a twin is a lot of fun!" one woman was saying.

"There's always someone to play with," said a little boy, putting his arm around his twin's shoulders.

"Yes, we swap clothes all the time," said a teenage girl.

"And we play practical jokes on our friends," added a man with a grin.

"We did it!" cheered Lila, spinning giddily into the air.

"Come down," said Myla, giggling at her twin's excitement. "Someone will see you! Besides, we have to take Rachel and Kirsty home."

Lila came down, laughing, and in a flurry of golden twinkles they were all transported back to Rachel's yard. They

heard Mrs. Walker's voice calling from
the back door of the house. "Rachel!
Kirsty! It's time to get ready for the
party!"

Lila and Myla each gave Rachel and
Kirsty a delicate kiss.

"Without you, we wouldn't have found
our magic objects," said Myla. "Thank
you so much."

"Good-bye, and thank you," said Lila. "Remember us, and have fun at the party!"

Waving happily, they vanished, leaving a little cloud of fairy dust hanging in the air.

"Look!" exclaimed Rachel, pointing at the wooden swing.

Two pink velvet boxes rested on the seat. One was marked KIRSTY and the other RACHEL in golden letters.

"They must be presents from Lila and Myla," said Kirsty.

The girls opened the boxes and saw
two halves of a pendant on long silver
chains, exactly like the ones that Lila
and Myla shared.

"How beautiful," Rachel exclaimed.
"We can wear them at the party."

They fastened the pendants around
their necks and smiled at each other.

"Rachel, do you ever wish you had
a twin?" Kirsty asked.

Rachel smiled and shook her head. "I have someone just as wonderful as a twin," she said. "I have the best friend in the world!"

Kirsty grinned and gave Rachel a hug.

THE MAGICAL CRAFTS FAIRIES

Don't miss any of Rachel and
Kirsty's other fairy adventures!
Join them as they try to help

Kayla
the Pottery Fairy!

Read on for a special sneak peek . . .

Crafts Week

"I can see Rainspell Island!" Rachel Walker cried as the ferry sailed across the blue-green sea, foamy waves slapping against its sides. Up ahead was a rocky island with soaring cliffs and sandy golden beaches. Rachel turned to her best friend, Kirsty Tate, with a smile. "It's not far now."

"Aren't we lucky, Rachel?" Kirsty asked, her face bright with excitement. "We visited here not that long ago for the music festival, and now we're back again for Crafts Week!"

"And maybe some fairy adventures, too?" Rachel whispered hopefully.

"Maybe . . . if we're *really* lucky," said Kirsty with a grin.

The ferry docked at the pier, and the girls' parents came up from belowdecks with all of their bags.

"That's our taxi," said Mr. Tate, pointing out a car waiting on the pier.

Before long, they arrived at Daffodil Cottage, a pretty little house with a thatched roof.

"Mom, can I go over to the campsite

with Rachel?" Kirsty asked as the taxi driver unloaded their bags.

"Of course," Mrs. Tate replied. "We'll come and pick you up later."

The campsite was a little farther down the road, in a large field. When they arrived, Rachel and Kirsty jumped out of the taxi, thrilled to see that Mr. and Mrs. Walker had rented one of the biggest tents on the site.

"Rachel, why don't you and Kirsty head into town and find out more about Crafts Week?" Mrs. Walker suggested. "Your dad and I will unpack."

"OK," Rachel agreed.

The girls left the tent and hurried across the field. The town wasn't very far away at all—in fact, they could see the rooftops in the distance. They climbed over a small fence and then wandered down a twisting country lane.

"I always get the feeling that something magical is going to happen on Rainspell," Kirsty said dreamily.

"That's because it always does!" Rachel laughed.

RAINBOW magic ™

Which Magical Fairies Have You Met?

- ❑ The Rainbow Fairies
- ❑ The Weather Fairies
- ❑ The Jewel Fairies
- ❑ The Pet Fairies
- ❑ The Dance Fairies
- ❑ The Music Fairies
- ❑ The Sports Fairies
- ❑ The Party Fairies
- ❑ The Ocean Fairies
- ❑ The Night Fairies
- ❑ The Magical Animal Fairies
- ❑ The Princess Fairies
- ❑ The Superstar Fairies
- ❑ The Fashion Fairies
- ❑ The Sugar & Spice Fairies
- ❑ The Earth Fairies
- ❑ The Magical Crafts Fairies

📖 SCHOLASTIC

Find all of your favorite fairy friends at
scholastic.com/rainbowmagic

HIT entertainment

RMFAIRY11

RAINBOW magic™

SPECIAL EDITION

Which Magical Fairies Have You Met?

3 stories in each one!

- ☐ Joy the Summer Vacation Fairy
- ☐ Holly the Christmas Fairy
- ☐ Kylie the Carnival Fairy
- ☐ Stella the Star Fairy
- ☐ Shannon the Ocean Fairy
- ☐ Trixie the Halloween Fairy
- ☐ Gabriella the Snow Kingdom Fairy
- ☐ Juliet the Valentine Fairy
- ☐ Mia the Bridesmaid Fairy
- ☐ Flora the Dress-Up Fairy
- ☐ Paige the Christmas Play Fairy
- ☐ Emma the Easter Fairy
- ☐ Cara the Camp Fairy
- ☐ Destiny the Rock Star Fairy
- ☐ Belle the Birthday Fairy
- ☐ Olympia the Games Fairy
- ☐ Selena the Sleepover Fairy
- ☐ Cheryl the Christmas Tree Fairy
- ☐ Florence the Friendship Fairy
- ☐ Lindsay the Luck Fairy
- ☐ Brianna the Tooth Fairy
- ☐ Autumn the Falling Leaves Fairy
- ☐ Keira the Movie Star Fairy
- ☐ Addison the April Fool's Day Fairy
- ☐ Bailey the Babysitter Fairy
- ☐ Natalie the Christmas Stocking Fairy
- ☐ Lila and Myla the Twins Fairies

■SCHOLASTIC

Find all of your favorite fairy friends at
scholastic.com/rainbowmagic

HIT entertainment

RMSPECIAL14